INTRODUCTION:

Phenylketonuria, also known as PKU is a Genetic Metabolic Disease in which the body cannot break down an amino acid called Phenylalanine, which is found mostly in foods that contain protein. There is no cure. This book series is to spread awareness, and open a conversation to other metabolic diseases. The world is full of unique and extraordinary people. Our hope is that these books will open your mind, and your hearts, for families with dietary requests. And that a day may come that all of these requests will be met without judgment, but rather kindness and compassion.

Happy Valentines Day Frankie
Written and Illustrated by Kacie Foos

Hi! I'm Frankie and I love Valentines Day! It's one of my favorite Holidays. I love writing cards and delivering them to all of my friends and family. But this year is a little different because there was a Virus and a lot of people got sick. So to show that we all cared for each other, we all had to spend more time at home with our families.

Even my school was closed. Normally we have a really fun Valentines Day card exchange with my schoolmates. I even make one for my teacher every year. This year I knew I was going to have to do things differently.

Valentines Day for me, like all holidays can be a little tricky.

Because I have PKU, I have to follow a very special diet.

I drink a formula, and have to take frequent blood tests to make sure I stay healthy.

Many people around the world like to gift chocolate to their friends and loved ones. That is one of the many things I can't eat because it has too much protein in it. Thanks to a medicine I take I am allowed to have four grams of protein a day. So for Valentines day I like to make cards and give my friends PKU friendly treats.

In just 1 oz of milk chocolate there is 1.4 grams of protein.

I thought about how I could spread love and kindness to my friends and family this year.

Cupid must have struck me with an arrow because suddenly I had the best idea!

I told my Mom and we got on the computer and asked a PKU parent group if anyone was interested in doing a Valentines Day card exchange.
Instantly we started getting replies from all around the world!

I was so excited. I started making Valentines right away. I thought about all the names I was writing on the cards, and all of these friends I had never met before that had PKU just like me. I imagined meeting them all some day.

My Mom and Dad helped me get all of my envelopes addressed and stamped and we were off to the Post Office drop box. I mailed fifty Valentines all together! Every Valentine I mailed I made a special wish for that new friend.

I checked the mailbox every day. But no
Valentines had arrived for me.
I started to feel really sad. I thought maybe
everyone had forgotten about me.

I put an X each day on the calender counting
down to Valentines Day. It was the thirteenth
and still no Valentines. My parents told me to be
patient and no matter what happens that I
should be happy knowing that I had done
something very kind for others. I knew they were
right but I still felt forgotten about and sad.

Valentines Day had finally arrived! My Daddy surprised me with some beautiful flowers and asked me, "Will you be my Valentine, Frankie?" I told him "Always."

That day my Dad surprised my Mom with a grand romantic gesture. He lead her into the backyard where he had engraved their initials in our tree. He then pulled out a piece of paper. He explained that he had gotten us a trip to ITALY for when it was safe to travel again. My Mom cried "happy tears" all day. I love seeing how much my parents love each other.

I checked the mail all day but still no Valentines. Right when I was about to give up, "DING DONG" the doorbell rang. I opened the door to find Harold, our friend and mailman, standing with a huge bag. "Frankie Foos, I have a Valentines Day delivery for you!" I couldn't believe it! I had never seen so much mail in my entire life!

My Dad helped carry the bag into our living room
and dumped mail all over the floor. I read
Valentines all day from all over the world. Some of
my favorites were the Valentines I received with
pictures from kids with PKU just like me.

Happy Valentines
Day
Frankie
♡ , Bella
& CARSON

As if this day couldn't get any better, my parents arranged a big Virtual Valentines Day get together with our family on the computer. We drank PKU friendly Sparkling Strawberry Lemonade and we all got to catch up and share quality time together.

HAPPY VALENTINES DAY EVERYONE!

Frankie's PKU Friendly

SPARKLING STRAWBERRY LEMONADE

Ingredients
1 Cup of Water
1/2 Cup Granulated Sugar
1 Cup Freshly Squeezed Lemon Juice
2 Cups of Strawberries, stems removed
4 Cups Sparkling Water

RECIPE

1) In a Medium Saucepan, bring 1 Cup of water to a boil. Add sugar until its dissolved. Stir in lemon juice and remove from heat. Let mixture cool completely.

2) Blend 1 and 1/2 Cups of Strawberries until smooth.

3) Whisk strawberry puree, sugar mixture, and sparkling water together in a large pitcher.

4) Place in refrigerator until completely cool

5) Slice up remaining strawberries and add to lemonade. Add ice and serve!

Have More Fun with FRANKIE!

"Frankie's Malibu A PKU Friendly Adventure"
"Frankie's London A PKU Friendly Adventure"
"Frankie's Paris A PKU Friendly Adventure"
"Frankie's Maui A PKU Friendly Adventure"
"A-Z with Frankie A PKU Friendly Learning Book"
"Frankie's Halloween A PKU Friendly Holiday"
"Frankie's Christmas A PKU Friendly Holiday"
"Happy Birthday Frankie"
"Frankie Goes To Summer Camp A PKU Friendly Adventure"

"WILL YOU BE MY VALENTINE, FRANKIE?"

"ALWAYS"

CPSIA information can be obtained at www.ICGtesting.com
Printed in the USA
LVIW011908170221
679383LV00004B/15